MW01232910

Grace Given

A Novella

Craig C. Sapp

authorHOUSE®

AuthorHouse™
1663 Liberty Drive, Suite 200
Bloomington, IN 47403
www.authorhouse.com
Phone: 1-800-839-8640

First published by AuthorHouse 1/6/2009

ISBN: 978-1-4389-3289-7 (sc)

Printed in the United States of America
Bloomington, Indiana

This book is printed on acid-free paper.

Acknowledgements

*F*irst and foremost, I want to thank my Jesus, for giving me the opportunity to live for Him, as my Savior, and as my Father, and as my Helper, and as my Friend, and as my Master…as my all in all. Jesus, I love You! Thank You!

To my wonderful wife, Caroline. Honey, you are not perfect, as none of us are, but you're close enough to perfect for me! I LOVE YOU SO VERY MUCH, CAROLINE! Thank you!

I also want to thank my sister, Angie Jacobs, for the encouragement and for the editing help that you have given me. Angie, I love you! Thank you!

Next, my sister Amie Busbee. Amie, you might not realize this, but there have been so very many times that you have been an inspiration to me! Amie, I love you! Thank you!

My mother and father, Carson and Madeline Sapp. What can I say? Mom, even though Daddy is at home with our heavenly Father, you continue to provide me with so very much love and support, and I thank you and Daddy both for giving us children a Christian home and environment in which to live. I love you, Momma! Thank you!

Dr. Tab Smith. Brother Tab, I remember the day I went to yours and Mrs. Betty's house and asked you to be my spiritual mentor, and you agreed without hesitation. You have done a wonderful job, and I truly believe that God is using you to help conform me to the image of His Son, Jesus Christ. I know that I will never be that image as long as there is breath in this body, but you help me to remember that He who began a good work in me will indeed see it through to completion. Holy mackerel, I thank you, Brother Tab!

Wes LeRoy, you have guided me through the publication process. Thank you, my brother!

If I were to thank all of the people who have had a part in my development and in this book's development, I am certain that I would miss some, or many, ones. So I want to thank everyone who I have ever had any contact with, as each and every one of you have played a part in my becoming who I am and will be. Thank you!

Preface

The following is a work of fiction. It is occasionally loosely based on some situations in the lives of people that I am very close to, but it is indeed fiction. Those who know me best may see circumstances and references to things that seem familiar, but rest assured; all names have been changed.

I ask you, the reader, to do this. If you begin reading this book, read it to its completion! There are many messages in this book, and there is an *overall* message in the book as a whole. Please, I ask you, if you begin it, finish it.

If anyone in this world is offended in any way by something that I have written here, please know that is not my intention. If anyone is offended by any of the Scripture quoted here, you will need to talk to God about that, because all Scripture quoted is His inspired Word!

God bless you, beloved!

Craig C. Sapp

Chapter 1

*J*ohn Paul Smith was born in a small town in Georgia, to his parents, William Carson and Madeline Kathryn Smith. Carson and Madeline had planned throughout Madeline's pregnancy, once they found out John's gender, to name him Kyle Gregory. But on the day that John was born, Carson stuck his head in Madeline's room, and said, "Honey, can we name him John Paul instead? I have a feeling this boy is going to be a special ambassador for Jesus, and both John and Paul were, too."

Having just given birth to a healthy, nine pound, eight ounce baby, Madeline was in no mood to argue, so she said, "Whatever you think, honey."

Every Christian father hopes that his child will be an ambassador for Christ, but Carson Smith didn't realize just how prophetic his statement was.

Carson and Madeline Smith were both born again Christians, and they did, indeed, believe every word of the Bible as absolute truth. So they raised their child up in the way he should live, like Proverbs 22:6 suggests. But John didn't always live the way he should. In fact, John often seemed to do the *wrong* thing even when the *right* thing would have given him, immediately, better results. In his teenage and young adult years, you could have called John a rebel, and that still would have been putting it mildly.

John did finally, however, at the age of 23, receive Christ as his Savior. It still took a few years after that for John to accept Jesus as Lord, and since it really isn't possible to receive Christ completely as just one or the other, in those few years, John was very often unsettled, and had few times of peace. John moved to northern Michigan a few years after he gave Lordship of his life to Jesus, and he lived there for five years.

Then one day John received a telephone call in Michigan from his father, Carson, in Georgia. After initial small talk, Carson said, "John, I called for a specific reason today. I have been diagnosed with pancreatic cancer." It was June.

John did some research, and he quickly discovered that pancreatic cancer usually acts rapidly, and patients with pancreatic cancer normally spend most of their time suffering. John thought to himself, "Well, these people that I got all this information from apparently don't know my

God." Regardless, three days later, John was on an airplane back to Georgia.

John and his dad had become best of friends, as well as father and son. They had been business partners for eight and a half years before he moved to Michigan, and they had really become best buddies They had been through a lot together. So the time that they were together now was truly a blessing to John. The time was a blessing to Carson, too.

John frequently prayed to God concerning his dad. His prayers always went something like this: "Father, I come before you again with praise and thanksgiving. Abba, I thank You for another day of life with which You have blessed me. Father, I pray that You will heal Daddy, and don't let him suffer any more than is absolutely necessary, according to Your will. I thank You, God, and I pray these things in Your Son Jesus' holy, precious, and perfect name. Amen."

On October 3, Carson died and went home to be with Jesus. Less than four months after he was diagnosed with pancreatic cancer, William Carson Smith was dead. John knew that his mom and dad had been married for nearly fifty years, and that they were partners in life, and were indeed best friends. He had seen those two examples all of his life. So he decided to stay with his mom, Madeline, and be strong emotionally for her.

But inwardly and privately, John was having the natural human reaction: "Why, God? Didn't You hear my prayers? Why?" In one of these moments, it was almost as if John heard God say, "John, son, I did hear your prayers. Your daddy is here in heaven with Me now, and I didn't allow him to suffer much. And today, your daddy is one hundred percent healthy, completely healed. And you will indeed see your daddy again, John. I love you, son." And it was all true. Carson was on a tractor three days before he died, doing what he loved to do, and that was operating farm equipment, working the ground. He hadn't suffered much, especially as much is normal with pancreatic cancer.

Chapter 2

*I*t was a bright, warm day, full of sunshine. There wasn't one single cloud in the sky, and it was so blue that it was hard to believe that God allowed a sky so beautiful to be seen by human eyes.

John felt…well, he wasn't sure what he felt. He was unemployed, per se, although he was transcribing sermons that a friend of his, Dr. Octavius Miller, had taped years ago. Dr. Miller had been "retired" for quite some time, if preachers ever really retire, and had asked John to transcribe his recorded sermons for him. So John had *somewhat* of a job. He lived with his mother, Madeline, and he was single, so he didn't have a need for a lot of money, but he felt somehow incomplete.

Actually, transcribing the sermons by Dr. Miller was giving John invaluable insight into the Bible and its messages, and John was enjoying that very much. John had been ordained as an evangelist earlier that same year, and he did preach from time to time, when asked. But he was only asked every once in a while.

On this particular day, John decided to go to a Christian chat site online to "talk" to some of his brethren around the world. So he logged on to a site, chose what he thought was a witty nickname, and proceeded to chat with those in the chat room. Little did he realize how much this day would change his life.

John soon met a woman who said she was from Sweden, a Christian who wanted some feedback from other Christians concerning an idea she had. So she shared this idea with John. Although he had no point of relation to her idea, and he made that clear, she asked for his opinion anyway. So he gave her his Bible-based opinion, and she said, "Thank you very much."

"You are very welcome," he replied.

And that is how their conversation ended that day.

The next day, while taking a break from transcribing, John went back to the chat site, having enjoyed the fellowship he had shared the day before with brothers and sisters in Christ around the world. And then he saw this Swedish woman's nickname on the user board. He thought to himself, "I am sure glad that I only gave her my *Bible-based* opinion. I'm going to ask her where her thinking is on this today."

So he typed in the question, "What are your thoughts about your idea today?"

To which she replied, "I turned in my resignation yesterday after our chat."

See, here's the deal: this woman was a public prosecutor, and she was having mixed emotions about putting people behind bars. She felt a sense of accomplishment when she got a conviction of someone that she was sure was guilty, but sometimes, she got a person convicted that she *wasn't* sure was guilty. That was causing her grief. Apparently, she was good at what she did. And even in the convictions of the absolutely guilty, she was very well aware of the grace that God had given to her when she was saved, even though she was "absolutely guilty".

So when she shared these thoughts with John, and her thoughts about possibly resigning as a public prosecutor, John thought to himself, "I need to be very careful that I don't tell her what I would do, because I actually have no clue what I would do. If she asks, I'll be sure that she understands that the opinion I give her is based exclusively on what the Bible has to say concerning this situation in her life."

"You did WHAT?" John asked.

"I gave my resignation. I thought about the things you said, and made a note of the Bible references you gave me, and after I looked up and read and studied those references, I prayed to our Father, and then I resigned. It was quite simple, really." She was so very calm.

"Ma'am, pardon my inference here, but you just met me yesterday, and that was only online, not even in person. Why did you listen to what I had to say?" John asked.

"Don't flatter yourself too much. I *did* only meet you yesterday, and that only online, but I have been a child of God for some time, and He and I have been developing a relationship for a long time, and you gave me references to *His* words. I resigned after consulting with God's Word, and then consulting with God." He was beginning to understand how she could be so good at what she did.

"So what are your plans for a career now?' John asked.

"Well, I'm not absolutely certain, but of this I *am* absolutely certain: God will provide."

"Wow!" John thought. "This woman has a pretty good level of faith!"

Later he would learn that he had no idea how high her level of faith was.

Chapter 3

*I*t had been several months since John and the Swedish woman had begun chatting on the online chat site. She had accepted a job as a legal representative for a Swedish labor union, and John had started as the office manager for the ministry of which Dr. Miller was president. He and the woman had exchanged telephone numbers, and occasionally talked to each other on the phone. They were both content, and were becoming complacent, with their lives. But God appears not to be very fond of complacency.

John had learned some things about this woman, and she had learned some things about John. They had chatted on a regular basis, and one of the wonderful things about talking without seeing is that people get to know each other without appearance playing any part whatsoever in the relationship. She and John had become very good friends.

Her name was Damie Rod, and she had been Sweden's premier prosecutor before she resigned. Defense attorneys dreaded facing her in court.

Just days after her resignation from the County Prosecutor's office, she was contacted by the largest labor union in Sweden and offered a job to be the head of their legal department. She accepted the job, and since she was no longer putting people behind bars, and had a say in her representation in legal matters, she was much happier doing what she did now.

Damie and John were getting more comfortable in their relationship with each other. They had begun to share some personal aspects of their lives. They were falling in love. Finally, they decided, each to himself and to herself, to love each other. They didn't consciously realize this fact, but it was a fact, nonetheless.

One day, while on the phone, Damie said, "What do you look like? We have been communicating for a long time, and we have no idea what each other looks like."

Jokingly, John said, "Well, we will just have to meet somewhere face-to-face and remedy that!"

"Well, how about if I come to America for a visit?" Damie said.

Caught by surprise, John asked, "Are you serious?"

Damie said, "Yes. I very frequently *am* serious, and this is one of those times."

So they arranged for Damie to come to America for a visit. John wrote his computer nickname on a T-shirt with a magic marker since they had not seen each other, put the shirt on, and went to the airport to pick Damie up when she was to arrive.

This is what Damie saw at her first sight of John. He was about six feet tall, with an average build; he wasn't muscular, nor was he skinny. His eyes were bright, and appeared to be able to see past any walls that were put before him, figuratively speaking. He wore a contagious smile, and was eager to share it with everyone with whom he came in contact. He was handsome. Damie thought that he was the most beautiful man that she had ever seen.

This is what John saw at his first sight of Damie. She was slim and about five and a half feet tall. She appeared effervescent and very lively. Her eyes seemed to convey a sense of tranquility, yet her personality was very attuned. Her smile was radiant, exuding the Light than lived within her. She seemed to almost glow, and she really stood out in a crowd. She was a beautiful lady. John thought that she was the most gorgeous woman he had ever seen.

John and Damie continued to develop their relationship while they were together. They were so compatible that it almost seemed that they had known each other all of their lives. They were together for several weeks, and John decided it was time for him to step out on the proverbial limb. So John proposed marriage to Damie. Damie accepted.

They decided together that John would move to Sweden. John's mother had assured him that she was ready to live by herself. John knew nothing about Sweden, but he knew something about his God, and he knew that God causes everything to work together for good to those who love Him and are called according to His purpose. John had learned that even when situations and circumstances in his life appeared on the surface to be bad, God was conforming him to the image of His Son, Jesus Christ, so even the "trying" times worked together for his good.

John and Damie were married in a beautiful ceremony. The weather that day seemed, both to Damie and to John, to be the most perfect that they had ever experienced in their entire lives. It was indeed a gorgeous day, but a lot of that had to do with the joy the day held for them, as well. They were married in John's home church, where he had been worshiping God for many years. John had packed up his possessions and sent them ahead previously to Damie's home in Sweden. They spent a week on their honeymoon, and then began their lives together in Sweden.

John got a job at a small local publishing company. Damie continued her legal work with the labor union. God had indeed stirred up and activated John and Damie's complacent lives.

Chapter 4

Damie Rod was born in Norway, to two psychologists, Marie and Pierre Rod. Although neither was a Christian, they were relatively wholesome people, from a worldly perspective. So they raised Damie to know the difference between right and wrong. Damie had a happy childhood, but in her eighth year of life, her childhood took a drastic turn.

Marie and Pierre Rod had attended a convention concerning itself with the involvement of the human mind in the activities of the human body. It had been a very eye-opening convention in Germany, and now they were flying to Sweden to pick up Damie from Marie's mother's house, and then to return to their home in Norway.

When their airplane was over the North Sea, it developed engine trouble in one of the four engines. That engine eventually stopped working all together. Two of the remaining three engines soon developed trouble, and the pilot and co-pilot tried desperately to correct the problems, but to no avail. The pilot put out a mayday call over the radio. Soon after that, the airplane plunged into the icy cold North Sea.

Rescue specialists received the mayday call, and they made their way rapidly to the site of the wreckage. The airplane was in pieces. The rescue team only saved twenty-seven of the two hundred twenty-eight passengers that were aboard the flight. Marie and Pierre Rod were not among those rescued. They were lost at sea.

Marie's mother, Dorothy Escobar, was concerned, because her daughter was usually on time, and when she wasn't, Marie always notified her. Now she was over two hours late, and Dorothy had not heard from Marie. And Dorothy knew how much Damie meant to Marie and Pierre both. Damie had been the apple of her parents' eyes since the day she had been born. Damie was their only child, and she had never wanted for anything her entire life. And so Dorothy was indeed concerned.

Then there was a knock at the door. Dorothy answered it when she saw that it was a policeman, and a policeman that she knew.

Dorothy said, "Hello, Frank. Come in, won't you?"

"Thank you, Mrs. Dorothy," Frank replied.

Dorothy was not feeling good about this visit. "Frank, is there anything wrong with Marie and Pierre?" she asked.

"Mrs. Dorothy, I'm very sorry to have to tell you this, but the airplane that Marie and Pierre were on crashed into the North Sea. They have not been found." Dorothy fell down to the ground and cried. Frank picked her up, and said, "Mrs. Dorothy, I am so very sorry, but where is Damie?" Frank knew the Rod family well, as they had spent a lot of time at Dorothy Escobar's house. And he knew that Mrs. Dorothy was in no shape to tell Damie the news of her parents.

About that time, Damie came to the door of the living room. "Granny Dot, are you O.K.? What is wrong?" she said, as eight-year-old Damie saw her grandmother crying.

"Hello, Damie," Frank said, as he lowered Dorothy to the sofa.

"Hey, Mr. Frank. What is wrong with Granny Dot?" Damie asked.

Frank said, "Damie, I hate to have to tell you this, precious girl. Your mom and dad were on an airplane that crashed."

"Well, Mr. Frank, are they in a hospital close by?" Damie asked. She thought she knew what he was saying, but she was just hoping she was wrong.

"Damie, Sweetie, they haven't been found."

With that, Dorothy began to try to get herself under control, and she said, "Damie, come here, Honey."

Damie was in shock. She walked over to her grandmother. And in that walk of just a few feet, this eight-year-old little girl found an emotional strength that stayed with her most of the remainder of her life.

"Granny Dot, we have got to stay strong...for each other. You and I will be O.K. I can stay with you, and help you through this tough time. I love you, Granny Dot," Damie said, as she embraced Dorothy in a big hug. Dorothy was amazed at her granddaughter's concern for *her* well being in a time like this.

Dorothy had been a Christian for many years, and she attended church three times a week, more if the doors were open. She looked at Frank and said, "Frank, this is the amazing grace of God that is so often sang about in Christian churches."

Dorothy and Damie embraced for a long time.

Dorothy Escobar took Damie Rod in and raised her as her own daughter. That meant that Damie was exposed to the Gospel of Jesus Christ many times every week, as Dorothy read her Bible at home often, as well as attending church at least three times a week. At the age of twelve, Damie received Jesus Christ as her Savior and as her Lord, and, over the next six years, with her grandmother helping her, she developed a close relationship with Jesus Christ.

At the age of eighteen, Damie enrolled and was accepted in law school at the University of Denmark. She graduated magna cum laude, top of her class, five years later. Damie began her law career one month after that in the Swedish public prosecutor's office.

Chapter 5

*W*hen John moved to Sweden, he was reminded of what the word "cold" truly meant! He had lived in Michigan for five years, and the winters in Michigan were very cold and full of snow, but he had lived in Georgia for several years now, and cold, snowy winters had become a distant memory. But, John learned, living in Sweden with Damie, it is fun to be kept warm by the person you love romantically, and to do the same for them.

After moving to Sweden, John soon learned about a gift that God had given to Damie; she had the most astoundingly beautiful and strong singing voice he had ever heard. Damie was the lead singer of a Gospel choir in Sweden, and John went to hear them practice one day. What he heard brought tears to his eyes, because Damie and the rest of the choir obviously used their talents to praise and worship God, and it really moved John emotionally.

The choir had arranged to put on a public concert in one of the city parks, and there turned out to be around four hundred people attending. The choir set up a huge television screen behind them so that the whole crowd could watch them. At a point in the middle of the concert, the choir walked off the stage, and Damie remained on the stage alone. She sang the song "Amazing Grace", a cappella, without any instrumental accompaniment. As she began singing, the huge crowd grew completely silent. When she finished the song, the crowd gave a standing ovation that lasted for several minutes. It was a truly moving rendition of that song.

Damie walked offstage, fell into the embrace of John, and a man very soon approached them from the audience.

"Sir, Ma'am, my name is Wayne Criswell. I am an American record producer for a company named Grace Given Record Company. Ma'am, I have been producing recordings of music for twenty-four years, and I have never heard a voice as completely beautiful as yours. I have hand-written a contract on my notepad to reserve your voice for Grace Given Records. If you will sign this basic agreement, we can work out the legal details later."

After learning a bit more about Wayne Criswell and his company, Damie, with John's unrestrained blessings, signed the contract.

This is how Wayne Criswell fell into the picture. Wayne owned a company called Grace Given Record Company.

He had owned this company for over twenty-four years. As you may assume from the name of his company, he was a Christian. Wayne and his wife, Betty, were taking a vacation in Sweden, and they saw in the local newspaper that there was going to be a public Christian concert, in English, at a park close by their hotel. They decided to attend. When they got to the park, they saw that several hundred people had shown up.

"This choir must be well known," Wayne said to Betty.

Soon after the concert started, Wayne remarked to Betty, "Honey, it does my heart so good to see people using their talents and gifts to praise and worship God! The entire choir is wonderful, but that woman singing lead is very, very gifted."

Then Damie started singing "Amazing Grace." During the first verse, Wayne took the notepad out of his shirt pocket, and began writing very fast. Betty wasn't *certain* of what was happening, but hearing the voice of the woman on stage, she had a pretty good idea. Wayne finally stopped writing, and when Damie finished the song, he said to Betty: "I'll be back in a little while."

So, it seemed that God wasn't going to allow John and Damie to be complacent now, either. John and Damie both returned to their day jobs the following Monday, but Damie was now under contract with Grace Given Records to produce five CDs over a period of seven years. God was using them both in many ways. John was being asked to preach at different churches every two or three weeks. And he had been asked by a couple of groups to lead revival services under tents, as well. Damie was translating his sermons from English to Swedish so that people that spoke one language or the other could hear the Word of God and the message of God in their own tongue.

And Damie was developing a friendship with a woman in her office named Elizabeth Moder.

Chapter 6

$\mathcal{E}$lizabeth Moder was a single woman. She was attractive, but had never allowed herself to get very personal with a man, nor had she allowed a man to get too personal with her. She had no children, but she had certain motherly qualities about her; she was compassionate, she was a caregiver, she listened when someone wanted to talk. She worked in the same office as Damie, and since Damie's mother had died when she was eight years old, and her grandmother when she was twenty years old, Damie sort of "adopted" her as her mother. And Elizabeth truly loved Damie's warm company, and since she had no children, Elizabeth sort of "adopted" Damie as her daughter.

There was something about Elizabeth that distressed Damie. That something was that Elizabeth was not trusting Jesus Christ as her Savior. Whenever Damie would bring up the subject of Elizabeth's salvation, Elizabeth would brush it off with some sort of comment along the lines of, "I try to live a good life. Now, I don't want to talk about that any more!"

Damie knew full well what the Bible says about the fact that we do not struggle against flesh and blood, but against spirits of evil. There were obviously demons that had enough of a hold on Elizabeth to keep her from turning her focus to the Savior. Many times, Damie tried to approach the topic of salvation with Elizabeth, but Elizabeth would always change the subject back to Damie, or to something else besides her own need for a Savior. As Damie prayed for Elizabeth one particular day, she got more desperate with God.

Damie prayed, "Father, Elizabeth is a person that I care for very, very much. I ask You to please, by any means necessary, draw her to You, as Your Word tells us must happen for us to come to Your Son. I ask this in Your Son Jesus' holy, perfect, and precious name. Amen."

The next day was a cloudy day, and Damie went to her annual routine check-up at her doctor.

"Hello, Damie. Are you having anything out of the ordinary happening today?" her doctor asked.

Damie smiled. "Not with my body, Dr. Casser, no."

Dr. Casser began her routine check. As she pushed on her stomach, she asked Damie, "Does that hurt?"

Damie replied, "No."

Dr. Casser continued to feel around her stomach, and Damie began to feel a little bit alarmed. "Is there a problem I need to know about, doctor?"

"I feel just a little abnormal bulge in your abdomen area. I just want to run a few tests, just to be on the safe side, O.K.?"

"Sure, Dr. Casser."

Dr. Casser drew some of Damie's blood to have it tested. She asked Damie, "Are you having any blood in your urine?"

"A little bit, but that just started, and it isn't very much at all."

Damie saw a scowl develop on Dr. Casser's face.

"Is that a need for concern, doctor?"

"Not automatically. We'll wait on the test results."

The next day, Dr. Casser called Damie herself.

"Damie, can you come to my office? Right now?"

"Sure, Dr. Casser. What is wrong?"

"Damie, don't be too alarmed. We'll talk about it when you get here."

Damie went immediately to Dr. Casser's office. Upon arrival, she was ushered in to her doctor's private office. Dr. Casser said, "Have a seat, Damie."

After sitting, Damie said, "All right, Dr. Casser, now what is wrong?"

"Damie, I have scheduled you for a CT scan. Right now. Your tests indicate that we need to test further. Now, there is still nothing for certain, so don't get beside yourself. I just want to test further as quickly as we can."

"Dr. Casser, you know me well enough to know that I am not too concerned with the circumstances and the changes of this life, but I am eager to know what the problem is. So let's do what is necessary."

"Good choice, Damie."

Damie was having a CT scan within two hours of that conversation with Dr. Casser. There was a radiologist on staff, so the results were read immediately.

Less than three hours had elapsed since Dr. Casser originally called Damie. Damie was seated in her office when Dr. Casser came in.

"Damie, you have a tumor on one of your kidneys. I want to send a biopsy for testing immediately."

Chapter 7

*I*t was raining when John got home from work, but he wondered what was making him feel uneasy as he entered his and Damie's house. Damie asked him to sit with her at the dining room table. She then proceeded to tell John the events of her day. John listened intently. He made not one sound while Damie told him all that had transpired that day.

When Damie had finished, the very first words out of John's mouth were, "Damie, kneel with me and let's pray together."

John prayed to God, "Our most kind and gracious heavenly Father, we come before you with praise and thanksgiving. Father, we thank You for this day of life that You have given us today. We thank You and praise You that you allow us to call You Father, and that You have adopted us as Your children. We love you so very much, God.

"Father, Your Word tells us to make our requests known to You. Abba, we are surprised by the news that

Damie received today, but You are not surprised at all. Father, I ask that you will reach down with Your healing hand and remove this tumor from Damie's body. But whatever You do, God, may it bring glory to You. You know the desires of our hearts, so there is no sense to try to hide the fact that Damie and I wish this tumor to be gone, but Your will be done, Father. We pray this in Your Son Jesus' holy, perfect, and precious name. Amen."

As they opened their eyes, both sets were filled with tears. Damie said, "John, I trust that God will be glorified in some way no matter what happens. And that fact gives me great joy. But I sure am glad that He allowed me to meet the Godly man that you are!"

She threw her arms around his neck, and they cried together for a long time.

Before going to bed, Damie called Elizabeth and asked her to meet her at their office a half hour early the next morning. She simply said that she had something that she wanted to talk to her about. Elizabeth agreed, and silently hoped that it was not about her salvation again. She was getting more and more uncomfortable when that topic came up in their conversations together. But she just agreed without reservation.

At the office, Damie was there when Elizabeth arrived. Elizabeth tried to detect what was on Damie's mind, but

Damie always seemed to have a sort of combination of love, joy, peace… Elizabeth couldn't seem to put her finger on it exactly, but there was a spirit about Damie that Elizabeth so much admired. She didn't know that she was seeing the fruit of the Holy Spirit that lived in Damie, as often as Damie tried to tell her. But Elizabeth did, in fact, see it in the life that Damie lived, even though she didn't know what it was exactly.

Damie didn't try to candy-coat the events of the day before. She simply told Elizabeth what had happened. Elizabeth was horrified, and her horror apparently showed. Damie said to her, "Do not be afraid for me, Elizabeth. I am not afraid for myself. I merely wanted you to know."

"But, Damie, you are such a good person! Call on your God!"

"Elizabeth, my relationship with God is the *reason* that I am not afraid. I have prayed that God will be glorified in this. To be completely honest with you, I have prayed that God will remove this tumor from my body, but first and foremost, that His will be done. I don't expect you to understand it all, but I think you need to be made aware of it all."

"Damie, thank you. You are correct, I do not understand it all, but I thank you for including me in your life."

They embraced for quite some time, crying together.

Dr. Casser called Damie later that day, and asked Damie to come to her office again. Damie called John and asked him to meet her at Dr. Casser's office as soon as he could. John and Damie met at Dr. Casser's office a few minutes later, and Dr. Casser asked them to have a seat.

"Damie, the biopsy showed that the tumor is malignant. You have cancer on your left kidney. I can schedule surgery for Tuesday, and I feel confident that it can all be removed with surgery. I am sorry to have to give you this news, Damie. I truly am."

"It is really O.K., Dr. Casser. God has a plan in this, as in everything. He is never caught by surprise!"

"Damie, my friend, your faith in God amazes me at times, and this is indeed one of those times!" Dr. Casser told her.

John looked at Damie with a look of disbelief, and smiled. "I second that, Dr. Casser!" John said.

Dr. Casser and Damie scheduled Damie for surgery the following Tuesday. It was Friday. John was preaching a tent revival that Sunday, and when Damie's news reached the revival organizers, they called John. "Brother John, if you want to not preach Sunday, we will find someone else to fill the pulpit."

"Nonsense!" John said. "This will be the best thing for me. Besides, I feel that God's Holy Spirit is really going to shake that poor old tent Sunday!"

Damie went back to the office and shared the news with the office staff. There were tears and many condolences given to Damie, and Damie got everyone to quiet down and she stood on a desk.

"I want everybody to hear what I am saying. I don't normally use my life situations and circumstances to get what I want, but today I want to give everyone in this office an invitation, and I do ask you to consider my situation as you think about my offer this time. John, my husband, is preaching Sunday, and I invite you all to come."

She proceeded to give directions to around twenty people, including Elizabeth. Damie had no idea what to expect.

Chapter 8

Sunday, the weather was a mix of rain and snow, but there was a pretty big crowd under the tent to hear John's sermon. In the crowd were seventeen of the nineteen people from Damie's office. She did not feel the least bit guilty, because she knew that if Jesus is *not* someone's Savior, then they *need* Jesus. And if He *is* someone's Savior, every Christian enjoys a good sermon from the Word of God! In the group, Damie was glad to see, was Elizabeth. And John preached the Gospel, as always. He presented it in a clearly understandable and practical way. He ended with the following story.

"Imagine with me that there is a two story house that is engulfed in flames. Firefighters have not yet arrived. By one of the second story windows stands a precious little girl. She is scared to death, and she is crying her eyes out. She cannot save herself. Without someone to save her, she will die.

"The first fireman on the scene is a big, burly fellow, and he hears the little girl's cries. He goes to the front door and finds it locked. He throws his full weight against it with all of his strength, and the door is ripped from its hinges. He goes inside to the stairway. The smoke and flames feel like they cook his lungs. He staggers up the stairs to get to the little girl. He comes to the room she is in and finds the door shut. He reaches out with his left hand and grabs the doorknob, and the blistering hot doorknob sears his left palm. He automatically snatches his hand back. Then he grits his teeth and grabs that doorknob with his right hand, and opens the door to the room that the little girl is in, and he reaches out to her with two damaged hands…

"Now, you write the rest of that story. Does the little girl throw her arms around the fireman's neck, and say, 'Thank you for saving me,' or does she turn her back and say, 'No thank you?'

"Around two thousand years ago, God Almighty left heaven and came to earth, becoming a Man, all by His own design. He allowed Himself to be arrested, unjustly tried, falsely convicted, horribly beaten, terribly humiliated, and then crucified on a barbaric Roman cross by nails being driven through His hands and His feet. He died, and was then buried, again, all by His own design. But in three days, He broke free from the grave, and He stood as he still stands today, in glory, offering salvation. He reaches out two nail scarred hands…to you.

"This is a true story where God allows you to write the next chapter. Will you reach out and take His hands and say, 'Thank You, Jesus,' or will you turn your back and say, 'No thank You?' Won't you come and receive Jesus, come and accept His offer of salvation? I will pray with you if you will come."

Many, many people came forward that day and received Jesus, including sixteen of the seventeen that were there from Damie's office. The one who did not come…Elizabeth. She stood with her eyes full of tears, and her cheeks wet from them, as well. But she did not come forward and receive Jesus as her Lord and as her Savior. Damie went to speak to her.

"I'm sorry, Damie, I'm sorry" was all she could say as she ran out of that tent.

The next day at the office, Damie went in as usual, and did not see Elizabeth. So after much shared prayer and well wishing, Damie went to the hospital to be prepped for surgery the next day. She was very disappointed not to have the chance to speak to Elizabeth, but she remembered that when she was a young girl, there seemed to be demons that tried to convince her not to accept Christ, in her mind, right before she submitted her life to Christ. She said a prayer specifically for Elizabeth.

Chapter 9

*E*lizabeth had lived a happy childhood. Her parents were Christians, and frequently taught her Bible stories, both about Jesus, God the Son, and about the miracles that God had performed in the lives of His people in the Old Testament, the nation of Israel. But when Elizabeth was fourteen years old, her parents were tragically killed in an automobile accident.

Elizabeth turned to alcohol to try to ease the pain of the loss of her parents. She had not accepted Jesus Christ as her Lord and Savior, and she tried to find a worldly solution to her problem of pain. She soon found what she thought was a solution to her problem of love, or better said, the lack of love, in her life. She turned to prostitution. She became deeply involved in a non-Christian lifestyle very quickly.

She learned a little about human nature throughout her remaining teenage and early-adult years, and she learned that human beings everywhere seemed to have a need for feeling loved, physically and emotionally. Elizabeth developed an attitude of compassion for people, and of a caregiver, and of listening when people wanted to talk.

Elizabeth left her life of prostitution because something about that lifestyle seemed morally wrong to her. She also came to the realization that her dependency on alcohol was unhealthy, so she turned from that as well and began living what she called a "good life", but she still felt like something was missing. She didn't realize that the void in her heart was shaped like Jesus Christ. He was what was missing in her life.

As Damie and John became a part of her life, they both talked about Jesus as if He was their personal Friend. So Elizabeth was feeling a very noticeable draw to God. She thought about God often, she listened intently when people talked about God, she even attended many Christian worship services, though she gripped the back of the pew in front of her until her knuckles turned white whenever an invitation was given to receive Jesus as Lord and Savior.

See, Elizabeth just didn't think that God would, or even *could*, forgive the "so very many sins" in her life. She didn't think that God was still the God of miracles.

Elizabeth hadn't read and studied the Bible in a very long time. She didn't remember that it was God's desire that we *all* be saved, and that *no one* should perish, as 2 Peter 3:9 tells us. Nor did she remember that God is omniscient, or all-powerful, and nothing is impossible for Him. She was now, however, being reminded of these facts about our Father, and her heart had begun to soften. She was getting close to believing that she could really be forgiven and saved from her sins!

Now, though, her close friend and "adopted daughter", Damie Smith, had cancer, and she thought to herself, "See! God can't do everything! Damie is such a very good person, a Christian, even! How can God let this happen to her?"

Elizabeth had suddenly become more confused than ever. She wasn't aware that one of Satan's most useful tactics is to put doubt in our minds, and therefore keep us as confused as possible. She still wanted to know the truth, but Satan tried his best to keep Elizabeth from finding it.

Chapter 10

The next morning, Elizabeth was in Damie's hospital room early, before Damie went for surgery. She apologized for not being at work the day before.

"I was sick. A group of wild horses couldn't have kept me away today, though!" Elizabeth told Damie.

"Or a group of demons," Damie thought to herself.

A little while after that, they came to get Damie for surgery. John prayed with her, and they took Damie away.

Elizabeth and John were the only two remaining in the room. Elizabeth said, "You did a wonderful job Sunday. I can't remember ever hearing God's plan for salvation given in such an understandable way."

"If you don't mind me asking, then what is keeping you away from God?" John asked.

"John, I have some very bad things in my past. For God to forgive me of those things would truly be a miracle. I just don't know if God still performs miracles like that." Elizabeth began to cry.

"So all you have to do is see a miracle?" John asked.

"Yes. If I *saw* a miracle, I would believe that God still *performs* miracles."

"I am not trying to be funny, but come with me."

He led Elizabeth to the window of the room full of newborn babies in the labor and delivery part of the hospital. "Elizabeth, what do you see here?"

"I see many babies," Elizabeth said.

"What did they do to get here?" John asked.

"Well, nothing, John. They were brought into this world…" Elizabeth paused.

"In a miraculous fashion, you mean?" asked John. "God still performs miracles, Elizabeth. God is the same today as He was yesterday, and He will be the same tomorrow."

"Mr. Smith! Mr. Smith!" John heard someone yelling his name. It was an orderly. "Dr. Casser sent me to find you! Come quickly!"

John ran, following the orderly, with Elizabeth not far behind. They met Dr. Casser in the hallway. Dr. Casser said, "John, when we opened Damie up to remove the tumor, we could not find a tumor! We cannot find a tumor, John! It's not there! It's a miracle!"

John turned to look at Elizabeth with his eyes full of joyful tears.

Elizabeth said, "John, I want to receive Jesus Christ as my Lord and my Savior right now!"

When Damie got back to her room from recovery, John and Elizabeth were there to greet her. Still groggy, Damie smiled at them.

John said, "Damie, say hello to your new sister in Christ!"

Damie began to cry. "Thank You, Father! Glory to You!"

Elizabeth leaned over Damie's hospital bed and said, "Our Father is indeed using the two of you in a mighty way. Now, Sweetie, you need to rest. But when you get out of this hospital, I will proudly do battle beside you in the army of God!"

With that, Damie drifted off to sleep.

When she woke, she opened her eyes and saw John smiling down at her. "John, I had a wonderful dream that Elizabeth received Christ as her personal Savior!"

At that point, Elizabeth walked out of the bathroom. "It isn't a dream, my dear Damie. It's a miracle!"

Chapter 11

$\mathcal{E}$ventually, Damie got back into the "routine" of her life, if it could be called a routine. Damie had learned that if she got complacent, look out, because it could very well mean that God was about to stir things up in a big way. But she went back to work for the labor union, with her new sister in Christ, Elizabeth, and got in touch with Wayne Criswell. She told him about the things that had recently happened in her life, and said, "Wayne, I fully realize now that I am indeed very special to God, and I want to get started soon recording my praise for Him."

Wayne said, "Great! How true your statement is. We are all very special to God! Now, let's first look at our options for locations to record. One possibility is that I do have a friend who has a small recording studio in Denmark. If he agrees to let us use it, that would be a better option for you than coming to America to record, wouldn't it?"

"Yes, it would," Damie said.

"O.K., Damie, then I will talk to him and get back in touch with you real soon."

John received invitations to preach more and more frequently. He was getting so many, in fact, that he had to turn some invitations down due to scheduling conflicts. He never imagined that he would get to this point.

John continued to preach the Gospel of Jesus Christ. In general, people everywhere that John preached seemed to realize their need for a Savior. "This is part of what God meant when He said that His Word would not return to Him void," John thought to himself.

When John first began preaching, he was very proud to proclaim the Word of God. But as John became more in demand to preach, he started getting proud more of himself. Soon, his messages began to reflect that pride. And soon after that, his invitations to preach diminished.

This was a crisis moment in John's life. He called his old friend and former employer in America, the president of the ministry that he had worked for, Dr. Octavius Miller.

"Hello," Dr. Miller answered.

"Hello, Brother Miller, this is John Paul Smith. How are you?"

"John! It is so very good to hear from you, friend! I am great! How are you and Damie?"

John briefly talked with Dr. Miller about the state of things in their lives, and then he said, "Dr. Miller, the reason I called today is that I want your advice. As I told you, I have in my recent past been asked to preach many times, but today I am not asked very often. Did you ever experience that in your preaching?"

"To be honest, John, I am still being asked to preach quite often, even though I have been 'retired' for many, many years. But there was a period of time in my life that I did experience what you seem to be experiencing."

"To what do you attribute the decrease in invitations to preach?" John asked.

"John, the problem, I discovered, was in the pronoun, so to speak," Dr. Miller responded.

"What do you mean?" John asked.

"I began to use the pronoun 'I' more than the pronoun 'Him'." Dr. Miller paused, and John pondered that statement a moment. "John, what I'm getting to is that it was becoming more about me and less about God instead of more about God and less about me, as John the Baptist put it."

"And what did you do to remedy that, Brother Miller?" John asked.

"I began to focus on the Word of God again," came Dr. Miller's simple reply.

"But, Brother Miller, some people don't seem to be as interested in hearing what the Bible has to say as they are in *arguing* about what it says. It is frustrating to me trying to defend the Bible! It takes away from the *message* of the

Bible!" John was starting to get his passion for the Word of God back.

"John, Charles H. Spurgeon is quoted as saying something along this line: the Bible needs for us to defend it no more than a caged lion needs us to defend it. We should merely let it out of its cage, and it will defend itself. Do you understand that?"

"I think so. I just need to present what the Bible says; let it out of its cage, so to speak, right?" John was getting his proper focus back

Dr. Miller said, "That's it. Always report what the Bible says, and do everything that you do for the glory of God."

"Thank you, Dr. Miller."

John was so glad to have a friend like Dr. Miller, a friend not afraid to be completely honest with him.

Chapter 12

*D*amie and Wayne Criswell worked out details with Wayne's friend in Denmark who owned the recording studio, Hugh Marks, and Damie started recording her first CD within a couple of weeks of coming home from the hospital. After getting the O.K. from Hugh, Damie invited Elizabeth to join her for a weekend in Denmark to give Elizabeth a break from her life in Sweden. Elizabeth was enjoying her life very much since she accepted Jesus as her Lord and her Savior, but Damie offered Elizabeth the opportunity to spend a weekend with her to give her some 'recharge' time, so to speak. Besides, Damie so very much loved Elizabeth! And the feeling was mutual.

When Damie and Elizabeth arrived at the Copenhagen airport in Denmark, they decided to stop at a café for a cup of coffee. After they sat down with their coffee, they noticed a woman a few tables away that was sitting with her head in both hands, talking to herself. She was sitting alone and was shaking her head back and forth. She lifted her head, looked at Elizabeth, and said, "How can life get so complicated?"

Not knowing the right thing to say, Elizabeth said, "Would you care to join us?"

The woman said, "O.K. Thank you."

The woman walked over and introduced herself. "My name is Annie," she said, and held out her hand to Elizabeth.

"I am Elizabeth."

"And I am Damie."

"Nice to meet you both," Annie said.

"Nice to meet you, as well," Damie and Elizabeth said, in unison.

This made them all three chuckle, "We're like two peas in the same pod, Annie!" Elizabeth said.

Damie chose to sit quietly and observe this time.

Elizabeth asked Annie, "Were you asking me that question for a response, or was that a rhetorical question?"

"Well…yes." Annie laughed. "If you don't mind, I would like to know what you think."

"Sure," Elizabeth said.

"I am a single mother. My son is fifteen years old. We have been doing O.K. to this point, but we are about to be evicted from our apartment, as I have recently lost my job and do not have money for rent. I don't know where to find the answers to life's questions, especially right now."

Elizabeth prayed silently, "Father, thank You for this opportunity! I ask You to guide me and lead me right now, so that You are glorified."

Elizabeth said to Annie, "If I told you that I knew where to find the answers to life's questions, would you think that I was a couple of sandwiches short of a picnic?"

Annie smiled. "Yes."

Elizabeth said, "Annie, do you know Jesus Christ?"

"Yeah, I know all about Him," Annie said.

"That is good, but that isn't what I asked you. Do you know Him personally?" Elizabeth asked.

"You can't really know Jesus personally!" Annie said.

"To the contrary, Annie. You *must* know Him personally!"

"What exactly do you mean, Elizabeth?" Annie asked.

Elizabeth was feeling so very bold proclaiming Jesus Christ. "Annie, the Bible reports in the book of John, chapter 14, verse 6, that Jesus said, 'I am the way, and the truth, and the life; no one comes to the Father but through Me.' What Jesus is saying to us is that the only way to God the Father is through accepting Him, Jesus Christ, God the Son, as our Savior and our Lord. Annie, do you realize that you are a sinner?"

"Boy, do I ever!" Annie said.

"So you do realize that you need a Savior from the consequences of your sins?"

"I guess I never thought about it. But yes, I suppose I would have to somehow be forgiven of my sins. My parents did teach me a *little* about the Bible," Annie said.

Damie thought to herself, "Or is it that you only *learned* a little of what they taught?"

Elizabeth said, "Annie, when Jesus came to earth, He came not to judge sinners, but that through Him, sinners might be saved."

"How does that happen?" Tears began to fall down Annie's cheeks.

"Thank You, Father! This seems to be progressing according to Your plan!" Damie prayed silently.

"Annie, I want to be sure that I understand what you are feeling and saying. You admit that you are a sinner, and that you need a Savior, right?" Elizabeth asked.

"Yes," Annie said, now sobbing freely.

"Annie, close your eyes and say a prayer like this one…"

Annie interrupted. "Right here, right now?"

Elizabeth said, "Annie, the Bible says that *now* is the acceptable time, and *today* is the day of salvation."

"Wow!" Damie thought to herself. "She *has* been studying the Bible!"

Annie said, "O.K., sorry. Go ahead…"

"No problem, Annie. Pray a prayer like this with me, with complete sincerity: 'God, I am a sinner. I know that

Your Son, Jesus Christ, came to earth, where He lived, He died, He was buried, and then three days later, He was resurrected, all so that *my* sins could could be forgiven. God, I accept Jesus Christ as my Savior and as my Lord right now. Father, I ask You to forgive me of my sins, and I ask You to show me how to live a life that is pleasing to You. Thank You, Father. Amen.'"

"Wow!" Annie said.

"What is it, Annie?" Elizabeth asked.

"I have never felt like this!" Annie said.

Damie said, "Annie, you are feeling the peace *of* God that we can only have when we have peace *with* God."

"But how do I get the answers to life's questions?"

Damie looked at Elizabeth, and Elizabeth gave her a nod. Damie proceeded. "Annie, now that you are a child of God, He will hear your prayers. A good thing to remember as you study the Bible, Annie, and I strongly suggest that you do that, is that in the New Testament, after the first four books, most of the rest of the New Testament is written to the children of God. By the way, we are all three now sisters in Christ! But in the book of James, chapter one, verse five, it is written, 'But if any of you lacks wisdom, let him ask of God, who gives to all generously and without reproach, and it will be given to him.' Now, understand this, Annie. When the pronoun is of the male gender in the Bible, it *often* refers to all children of God, not just men. That is the case here. So, ask God for His wisdom and He will give it to you, His child!"

They all three exchanged their contact information, phone numbers, email addresses, and the like, and then parted ways.

Damie told Elizabeth, "I am so very proud to have you as my sister in Christ! You did a wonderful job!"

Elizabeth said, "Well, sis, we'll keep each other encouraged as we go, how about that?"

Damie said, "Deal!"

Chapter 13

Damie soon finished recording the first of five CDs for Grace Given Records, quickly followed by the second and third. In the following months, Damie's CD sales were incredible. Damie was getting paid pretty big royalty checks, and she was feeling somewhat guilty for receiving them. One night, Damie told John, "I really don't feel as though I should be paid at all for my recordings. I am praising and worshiping Almighty God, and I'm getting paid for it! Something doesn't seem right about that."

John replied, "Honey, in the past, I have felt the same way about preaching, so I decided I would see if the Bible had anything to say about that subject, and as it turns out, it does! In Matthew chapter ten, Jesus gives instructions to the twelve disciples that he is sending out for the first time. He covers lots of topics in this chapter, but in verses nine and ten, He instructs them as to what to take on their journeys, and Jesus says, 'Do not acquire gold, or silver, or copper for your money belts, or a bag for your journey, or even two coats, or sandals, or a staff; for the worker is worthy of his support.'"

"Help me understand this, Sweetie," Damie said.

"O.K. First of all, Jesus is sending them out to the 'house of Israel'; in other words, to those who belong to God. Incidentally, in verse eight, Jesus says, 'Freely you have received, freely give,' but don't let that confuse you. Jesus is saying for us to freely give of that which we have freely been blessed with; our gifts, our knowledge of how to be saved and spend eternity with God, and those types of things. But what Jesus is saying in verses nine and ten is that someone who does the work *of* God *for* God is worthy to be supported for *doing* God's work. Damie, when you use your God given gifts to show to Christians how to give glory to God using those gifts, then you are worthy of the support that you receive for doing it. Now, your stewardship *with* that support is another topic."

"John, if you aren't careful, someone might accuse you of being a preacher!" Damie said. John smiled.

John smiled even bigger when Damie kissed him.

The phone rang at the Smith house.

"Hello," Damie answered.

"Damie, it's Elizabeth. I feel so ashamed, but I am having doubts about my salvation. I do believe what the Bible says to be absolute truth, but I am just having thoughts that I have no reason, that I can see, to have. Can I come over?"

"By all means! Come right away!" Damie said.

Damie got her Bible and waited for Elizabeth to arrive.

When Elizabeth arrived, she asked Damie if she had told John about her phone call.

"No, what starts between friends stays between friends, unless you say otherwise, Elizabeth," Damie said.

"Thank you, Damie! You are so very sweet to me!" Elizabeth said.

"Elizabeth, you can pay me later." Damie joked. "But let's begin with prayer, O.K.?"

"I would love that!" Elizabeth said.

Damie prayed, "Father, we come before Your throne with praise and thanksgiving once again. Father, I thank You first for creating us, and also, Father, for staying involved in our lives. God, I ask You to keep Satan and his demons away from Elizabeth and me while we get a clearer understanding of our assurance of your salvation given to us. Father, as we learn more about what You have taught us, we ask that You lead us into all truth, as You have promised. God, we thank You again, and we want You to know that we love You. We pray these things in Your Son Jesus' holy, precious, and perfect name. Amen."

Elizabeth said, "Damie, how do you know *what* to pray when you pray?"

"Elizabeth, our relationship with Jesus has this much in common with any relationship that we have: there are no short cuts. Our time of salvation is the *finish* line of our life *before* Christ, but, girl, it's just the *starting* line of our life *with* Christ! And keep this in mind; we have 'from here to eternity' to develop our relationship with Christ, to use the title from the old movie! We can get closer to Him every day. In fact, we should! And with the Holy Spirit's help, we can talk to God just like I am talking to you, and do so in a manner that He tells us to in His Word," Damie said.

"Then why do I have doubts?" Elizabeth asked.

"Elizabeth, doubt is to our soul what pain is to our bodies, so to speak. It lets us know something is wrong. Pain does not mean you are dead, pain means you are *alive*! And like pain, doubt is not usually permanent. Once we fix whatever is causing our pain, it usually goes away. It's the same way with doubt. Let me quote two Scriptures to you, Elizabeth. First, in 1 Peter 5:8, it is written, 'Be of sober spirit, be on the alert. Your adversary, the devil, prowls around like a roaring lion, seeking someone to devour.' What Peter writes to us here is that the devil never stops trying to lead us away from our Lord and Savior; he constantly "prowls around". Secondly, in Mark 9:24, it is written, 'Immediately the boy's father cried out and said, "I do believe; help my unbelief."' This is in the account of Jesus casting an unclean spirit out of this man's son. In the same breath, so to speak, the boy's father told Jesus that while he did in fact believe, he knew that there would be times of doubt, when his belief could be greater; so he asks the Master to help him with his unbelief. Elizabeth, whenever you have doubts, ask Jesus to help you with them."

"Oh, my dearest Damie, when did you get so wise? You are so young compared to me!" Elizabeth asked.

"In Psalm 111:10, we are told that the reverent fear of the Lord is the beginning of wisdom. Continue to develop your relationship with God, Elizabeth; all glory to Him!" Damie said.

"O.K., I'm confused. Is it you or your husband that is the preacher?"

That made them both laugh.

Chapter 14

John was preaching now almost every weekend. And he began to be concerned that his calendar remained full for speaking engagements. But he was finding that people didn't always *want* to hear the Gospel message of Jesus Christ. He had already learned that people didn't want to hear about him, either. People *wanted* to hear what made them feel good, so John began preaching more of a "name it and claim it" gospel. And his schedule for speaking soon became packed to capacity. And he was getting worldwide recognition.

Then one day, John's phone rang. John thought to himself, "I have to get a full-time secretary!"

"Hello!" John answered sharply.

"John, this is Brother Octavius Miller," came the reply.

"Dr. Miller! What a nice surprise! How are you?" John asked.

"I am doing fine, John. How is Damie?" Dr. Miller asked.

"She is very well, thank you for asking. Is anything wrong, Dr. Miller?" John asked.

"John, several months ago, you called me concerning your preaching. Today, I am calling you concerning your preaching."

John said, "Oh, Dr. Miller, everything is going wonderful with my ministry! I am preaching every weekend, and I often have worldwide television coverage of my messages. You should check them out sometime!"

"That is the reason for my call today, John. I have. And brother, because I love you, and because we are fellow preachers of the Word of God, I want to talk with you about 'your' sermons," Dr. Miller said.

"Everything is right about my sermons, Dr. Miller!" John said defensively.

"John, let me point out a few things. The first thing is, I love you very, very much. I want you to be completely sure that you understand that."

"Of that I have no doubts, Dr. Miller"

"Great. The second thing is, in this conversation, I have noticed something to this point. You used to call me 'Brother Miller,' but today, you insist on my formal title, 'Dr.' Why is that?"

"Well, Brother Miller, I just thought that would be what you would prefer to hear," John said, puzzled.

"That brings me to my third point, John. The sermon that I heard you give was what 'tickled the ears' of your listeners. Son, that will not do. You are an ambassador for Christ, as 2 Corinthians 5:20 says. As Christ's ambassador, we or to neither add to nor take away from His message to people. And remember what is written in Galatians 1:8? That if we, or *an angel from heaven*, preaches to you a gospel different than the Gospel of Jesus Christ, *he is to be accursed*!" Dr. Miller said.

Because Dr. Miller was such a faithful friend and such an insightful mentor to John, he took time to ponder this.

"Son, do you remember in 2 Timothy 4:3, Paul warned of the coming day that people will not endure sound doctrine, but instead will accumulate for themselves teachers who teach according to their own desires?" Dr. Miller asked.

"Yes, I do, Brother Miller," John said.

"John, earlier you called this ministry 'your' ministry. Always keep in focus that God is allowing you to be an ambassador in *His* ministry; and don't preach *your* messages, but rather the messages that the Holy Spirit urges you to preach," Dr. Miller said.

There was silence on the line for at least a full minute.

Then John said, very humbly, "Brother Miller, I so much appreciate your call today. I hadn't consciously realized that I had fallen so deeply into one of Satan's traps. It goes back to the problem with the pronoun, doesn't it? But what Satan intends for evil, God will use for good! If I weren't popular enough to be televised worldwide, you may have never heard one of 'my' sermons, and I would have gotten deeper and deeper into this trap. Thank You, Father, and thank you, Brother Miller, for not allowing that to happen!"

"And I thank you for taking this call for its intention. I love you, John!" Dr. Miller said.

John said, "I love you, too, Brother Miller!"

Chapter 15

"Damie, back up and give me room. I have an idea!" Wayne said.

Damie smiled. "What is it, Wayne?"

Damie had given up her career as a lawyer and was singing praise to God full time now, so she was at the recording studio regularly. Wayne had bought the recording studio from his friend, Hugh Marks, in Denmark, and after some renovations, had moved his headquarters there.

"Damie, have I ever shared with you that I have Type I diabetes?" Wayne asked.

"That's what is commonly called juvenile diabetes, right? No, you haven't, Wayne!" Damie was surprised by this news.

"You are right; it is commonly known as juvenile diabetes. I was diagnosed when I was five years old. And that has spurned my idea. Damie, I have been told for most of my life that a cure for diabetes is 'just around the corner'. I want to push research scientists closer to the corner," Wayne said. "Not necessarily for my sake, but I know the challenges that a child, not to mention an adult, with diabetes faces, and a cure would give them one less concern in their life. Or at least allow them to focus on a different one."

"O.K., Wayne. What is your idea?" Damie asked.

"To have a major fundraising concert for diabetes research, with Christian artists."

Damie thought about that for a moment. "Wayne, you know that I would be glad to help in any way that I can."

"I do know that, Damie, and I truly believe that others would be willing, as well. I wanted to run this idea by you first, because you are such a very wise woman. Not to mention the fact that you are so popular with everyone because of your gorgeous singing voice!"

Damie said, "I say we go for it!"

Wayne got in touch with the agents of close to thirty Christian recording artists about performing at a benefit concert for diabetes research. Out of those, he got agreements from six, seven counting Damie, performers to participate in this benefit. Wayne let his imagination run wild due to the fact that he had placed this entire endeavor at the foot of the Cross, and because of that, the popularity of the performers that agreed to perform. The list of artists included Clay Crosse, Third Day, Stephen Curtis Chapman, Michael W, Smith, Mercy Me, Casting

Crowns, and Damie Smith. After Wayne got those verbal agreements, he contacted the University of Michigan to see about the possibility of using their football field, known as The Big House, as the venue for this concert. It seats around 106,000 people. It turns out that the University of Michigan was eager to participate in this very large-scale concert, so details were quickly worked out.

"We should get a big name to emcee," Wayne said.

"Wayne, how about John? Not to say that he is such a big name, but he is a well known face who represents the Biggest Name, and he is, as I said, well known!" Damie said.

"Damie, do you think John would do it?" Wayne was excited.

"Well, Wayne, I *do* have a certain level of influence with Reverend John Paul Smith!" They both laughed.

John was delighted to agree to emcee this concert. When working out details with Wayne, John said, "One thing, Wayne; I would like to reserve the right to have a couple of minutes to comment between performers. Not a sermon, just comments!"

"You've got it, Brother! I have two run-throughs planned, so if your schedule allows, let's include you in those," Wayne said.

"It's a deal, my friend!" John said.

The day of the concert came, and it was televised on one of the national television networks. The weather was perfect for an outdoor concert, with a mix of sun and clouds, and the temperature was a warming eighty-three degrees Fahrenheit. The Big House was packed to capacity, and the network gave a toll free phone number to accept donations. The concert was a huge success. When all was said and done, there was over $3 million raised for diabetes research.

Wayne said, "Isn't it amazing what can be accomplished when we let God be in charge?"

Chapter 16

"Damie, I have a confession to make to you," Elizabeth said.

It was a gorgeous Saturday morning. The sun was shining brightly, and warming the earth nicely. Although Damie and John had moved to Denmark, and Elizabeth still worked for the labor union in Sweden, the two of them had developed such a close relationship that Damie would occasionally meet Elizabeth on Saturday mornings for breakfast. They were at Elizabeth's house.

"What is it, Elizabeth?" Damie asked.

"Damie, I have doubts about my salvation again," Elizabeth said.

"Elizabeth, get your Bible. We are going to settle your assurance of God's salvation that has been received *by you* once and for all," Damie told Elizabeth.

Elizabeth walked inside and got her Bible and brought it back outside.

"Turn to 1 John 5:13 and read that to me, Elizabeth," Damie said.

Elizabeth read, " 'These things I have written unto you who believe on the name of the Son of God, that ye may know that ye have eternal life, and that ye may believe in the name of the Son of God.'"

"Elizabeth, the Holy Spirit inspired Paul to write the words that follow so that you may *know* that you have eternal life!" Damie said. "Let's look at what the Bible tells us are the two things that do, in fact, save us. Turn to Ephesians 2:8-9 and read that to me."

Elizabeth read again, " 'For by grace are ye saved through faith, and that not of yourselves: it is the gift of God: not of works, lest any man should boast.'"

"First of all, what are we told here *doesn't* save us?" Damie asked.

Elizabeth replied, "Our works."

"Exactly. And how *are* we then saved?" Damie asked

"By God's grace through faith," Elizabeth replied.

"I think of it like this, Elizabeth. God reaches down to us with His grace, offering it to us, and we reach up to Him through our faith in Him, and receive His grace."

"Damie, you make so much sense!" Elizabeth exclaimed.

"All glory to God, Elizabeth, but let's not stop here. There are three tests we can use to know beyond the shadow of a doubt that we are children of God; the Lordship test, the Fellowship test, and the Relationship test. I want us to look at what the Bible says about these three tests," Damie said.

"Hold on, Damie!" Elizabeth said. "This is good stuff! Let me jot down some notes!"

"Take your time, Elizabeth, take your time." Damie smiled.

"O.K., Damie. Go ahead."

"Elizabeth, let's look at the Lordship test. Turn to 1 John 2:3-6 and read that to me," Damie said.

Elizabeth read again, " 'And hereby we know that we know Him, if we keep His commandments. He that saith, "I know Him," and keepeth not His commandments, is a liar, and the truth is not in him. But whoso keepeth His Word, to him verily is the Word of God perfected: hereby know we that we are in Him. He that saith that he is in Him ought himself also so to walk, even as He walked.'"

"Elizabeth, do you have a New American Standard Version of the Bible?"

"Yes," Elizabeth said.

"Would you get it?" Damie asked.

Elizabeth went inside and soon returned with a NASV of the Holy Bible.

"Because we don't use words like 'saith,' and 'keepeth' any more, the NASV is a trustworthy version in language more similar to that which we use today," Damie told her.

"Damie, this Scripture is exactly why I have doubt. I don't always keep God's commands. I strive to, but I don't always do it," Elizabeth said.

"Elizabeth, the word 'keep' here is a nautical term, like sailors used to 'keep' their way according to the stars. The ship may stray off course this way or that, but the experienced sailor always strived to 'keep' his course by the stars. In this analogy, think of God's commands as the stars by which we keep our course, so to speak. You are not saved because you 'keep' the commandments; you 'keep' the commandments because you are saved. A person who is born of God does not make sin her way of life. Are you getting my point?" Damie asked.

"Indeed I am, dear! You are so good!" Elizabeth smiled at Damie.

"I am married to a man who has helped me understand the Word of God so much better than I did! Have you met my husband John?" That made them both chuckle.

"Next, Elizabeth, let's look at the Fellowship test. Turn to 1 John 3:14-15, in the NASV, please, and read that to me."

Elizabeth read again, " 'We know that we have passed out of death into life, because we love the brethren. He who does not love abides in death. Everyone who hates his brother is a murderer; and you know that no murderer has eternal life abiding in him.'"

"O.K., now read John 13:35, Elizabeth," Damie said.

Elizabeth read again, " 'By this all men will know that you are My disciples, if you have love for one another.'"

"Elizabeth, when we are truly a child of God, we love what He loves, and God loves His children. Are you still with me?"

"Absolutely!" Elizabeth said.

"All right, now in closing, let's look at the Relationship test. Elizabeth, turn to 1 John 5:10-11, and read that to me."

Elizabeth read one more time, " 'The one who believes in the Son of God has the testimony in himself; the one who does not believe God has made Him a liar, because he has not believed in the testimony that God has given concerning His Son. And the testimony is this, that God has given us eternal life, and this life is in His Son.'"

"Elizabeth, as you know, a Christian is a person who has a relationship with Jesus Christ. As much as I love John, and our relationship is so very important to me, it is nothing compared to the priority of my relationship with Jesus. Remember to ask your Friend Jesus to help you any time you have a doubt, Elizabeth." Damie hugged Elizabeth.

"I love you and am so thankful for you, Damie!" Elizabeth told her.

"Well, then, how about considering becoming my personal assistant, Elizabeth? I mean, what better way to show your appreciation?" Damie smiled at Elizabeth.

"I have never considered such a thing, Damie! Where would I live, and what would I do for you, and what about my retirement income, and…"

"Elizabeth, I would take care of you. You have my word on that," Damie said.

"Well…O.K.…sold!"

Elizabeth began to cry.

Chapter 17

"*J*ohn, we can do *something*, can't we?" Damie asked.

Rain poured out of the heavens as if it was angry, but of course it didn't have emotions. It was just doing what we should all do, and that is what God told it to do. And God had apparently told it to fall rapidly!

Damie had just read of yet another horrible abduction that led to murder, involving a sixteen-year-old boy and a thirty-year-old woman, who had their original contact online. The young man had been murdered.

Because of the circumstances of their first meeting online, Damie somehow, oddly, felt responsible for the abductions relating to online relationships.

"Maybe, honey. I've been looking into that lately," John said. It had apparently been on his mind, as well.

John had been doing some legwork on an idea that he had concerning online protection for unsuspecting "chatters," as they were called. His premise of thought had been for some way to expose the real identities of online users. But recently, his thoughts had been changing.

"Damie, I believe that my thinking has been based on the wrong assumption. Up until now, it has been based on a symptom instead of the root problem. The abductions are a real and immediate and horrible symptom, but the fact remains that they are only a symptom. It has that in common with illegal drug use, I believe. It is my belief that they have the same root problem, in a general sense," John said.

To which Damie replied, "Please talk to me in language I can understand, John!"

"Damie, I truly believe that both of these 'symptoms' boil down to a parenting problem," John said.

"John!" Damie exclaimed.

"Face the reality, Sweetie. It is a built-in human desire to be loved by our parents. And to be corrected when we do wrong. And to be encouraged when we do right. While many parents of children do right by their children, there are very many who do not. Case in point, this thirty-year-old woman killed this sixteen-year-old boy. The article said that he lived alone, both of his parents having moved out of their house. When a child does not feel loved by their parents, they will look elsewhere. Satan knows that if he can drive a wedge in our basic family units, then he can work on the individual members of our families without our families operating as one unit, and then we are weaker." John continued. "It is my sincere belief that people like you and me, who have a little bit of influence with people, have the responsibility to somehow get the message to parents, and let the parents of the world know that they are to be held accountable."

"Change that to 'we,' darling," Damie said.

"What did you just say?" John asked.

"John, I'm pregnant."

John smiled so big that Damie thought his face would break. He ran to Damie and picked her up and spun around with her. Then he gently placed her back on the ground, and said, "I am so sorry! Are you hurt? Sit here on the sofa. Can I get you a pillow?"

Damie laughed. "John, I am only about three weeks along; I am fine! You act like I'll break like fine crystal!"

"My darling, you are like fine crystal, and you are carrying our fine crystal teacup!" John said. "This changes everything!"

"You don't mean about parents' responsibilities, do you?" Damie asked.

"No, that isn't at all what I meant, my love, but it does, in fact, change my perspective on that, too. I think I need to start delivering that message immediately! What I meant was that I will start planning my speaking engagements closer to home for the next ten months or so. And I..."

"John, don't forget the problem with the pronoun," Damie said.

John paused. "Thank you for that reality check, honey. You sit, and I will kneel, and let's pray," John said.

"John, I can still get on my knees, and I can't imagine a more appropriate time for me to do just that than right now." Damie got on her knees, and John knelt beside her.

John prayed, "Our most kind and most gracious heavenly Father, we do indeed come before You again with praise and thanksgiving. Father, I thank You for the gift of life that You have given us, and for the life of our child growing inside Damie right now. Thank You for trusting us with the life of one of your creations. Father, I ask that You keep both Damie and our baby safe and well cared for, and I ask You to show me how I can best serve You and them."

"Father, I have been having these thoughts about parents' responsibilities, and if it is Your will for me to move forward with a plan to deliver your messages concerning this, I ask You to guide me as You always do. Let me continue to be Your vessel, Father. God, if that is not the direction that You would have me go, I ask You to put my feet on the path where You would have me. Father

God, we love You so, so very much! We thank You again, and we pray these things in Your Son Jesus' holy, precious, and perfect name. Amen."

John said, "Damie, we're going to have a baby!"

Chapter 18

John, as was most often the case, went forward with his plan to get this message out to parents. He knew that the only way for God to *guide* our steps is if we are indeed *taking* steps. He frequently preached to congregations ranging in size between eight hundred and a thousand people, so very many people were at least *hearing* this message.

Here is a sample, a part of one of John's sermons.

"Ladies and gentlemen, today we need to think about something, and that is this thought. If we don't train our children in the way they should live, how will they know how they should live? No human being has ever had to train a child as to how to be evil, because that is the nature we are born into. In Genesis 8:21, it is written, '...for the intent of man's heart is evil from his youth...' And in Mark 7:21, Jesus is recorded as saying, 'For from within, out of the heart of men, proceed the evil thoughts, fornications, thefts, murders, adulteries'. So we are all born with thoughts of evil things as our destiny…unless we are taught otherwise. In Proverbs 22:6, it is written, 'Train up a child in the way he should go, even when he is old he will not depart from it.' As is always the case, there are many messages from every Scripture in the Holy Bible, but one of the many messages we are told here is to 'train up a child in the way he should go.' The message that God has put on my heart to deliver to us today is this: parents, it is our responsibility to train our children in the proper way to live."

After John gave this sermon, as usual, he waited in front of the pulpit to pray with those who came forward with prayer requests. John then gave a benediction to close the service, and a few people then came to him and wanted clarification of something he had said. "Preacher, did you intentionally include yourself in the group of parents?"

John said, "Wow! You guys really *do* pay attention, don't you?" He laughed. "Yes, Damie is pregnant. We are going to have a baby."

There followed that statement congratulation from everywhere. John was almost overwhelmed by the response of the people around him. Those people were genuinely happy for John and Damie.

Damie continued to record CDs under the Grace Given record label, and one day she was at the recording studio, along with Wayne. The two of them were sharing in small talk about their families, and Jamie said, "I think I am going to write a song about being a parent."

Wayne turned to look at Damie. "You mean you are pregnant?' he asked excitedly.

"Yes, I am proud to say, I am," Damie responded.

Wayne hugged Damie, gently, and congratulated her enthusiastically. He was so very happy for Damie and John.

"John, it is so peaceful to be in the center of God's will. I cannot think of anywhere I would rather be!" Damie was filled with both joy and happiness. God was really blessing this young couple because of their faithfulness to Him.

"Honey, I really don't believe that I could agree with you more!" John said.

Romans 8:28-29. "And we know that God causes all things to work together for good to those who love God, to those who are called according to His purpose. For those whom He foreknew, He also predestined to become conformed to the image of His Son, so that He would be the firstborn among many brethren."

Chapter 19

The very next day, Damie went to her gynecologist, Dr. Gloria Evans, to have her scheduled sonogram to check the status of their baby's growth. John and Damie had found out earlier that their baby was probably a female, and she was growing at the top of the charts.

They had been decorating her room and had been thinking about her name. Damie said, "What do you think about Hannah Rose, dear? I like that name."

John replied, "That is a beautiful name! We should keep that one on the short list!"

The sonogram technician said, "Hmmm…"

"What is it?" Damie asked.

"Just a minute. Let me get Dr. Evans in here."

She went to get Dr. Evans. Damie was a little bit concerned.

Dr. Evans came in the room. "Hello, Damie. How are you feeling?"

"I am feeling fine, but I am now a little bit anxious. Is there a problem?"

"Damie, there is no need to be anxious right now. Let me see what I can find in your sonogram," Dr. Evans said.

Dr. Evans ran the ultrasound transducer, the name given to the probe that is run over the abdomen, all over Damie's stomach. Dr. Evans then said, "Damie, we need to run additional test, because I can detect no heartbeat with this ultrasound machine. But don't be too alarmed; this machine is not always reliable."

Damie remembered Dr. Casser's comments when she had found a tumor on one of Damie's kidneys. They were eerily similar.

Dr. Evans continued testing, trying to find a heartbeat of the baby in Damie's stomach. After much testing, Dr. Evans left the room, saying, "I'll be right back, Damie."

Damie prayed, "Father, please let a heartbeat be detected!"

Dr. Evans returned. Her face showed no traces of her normal smile, in fact, no happiness at all. She looked Damie in the eyes. "Damie, your baby has gone home to be with our Father. I am so sorry."

Immediately Damie began sobbing, and cried out, "Why, Father, why!? God, please, no!"

Dr. Evans quickly said something to one of the nurses, telling her to call and gently tell John what was happening, and then she reached out to Damie. Damie fell into Dr. Evan's arms, and sobbed continuously for quite some time, and then John walked in. His eyes were bloodshot, and it was obvious that he had been crying, as well.

When Damie saw him, she grabbed him, and said, "John, why is God doing this to us? We both serve Him faithfully every day of our lives!"

John silently hugged Damie, and Dr. Evans got everyone out of the room and left them alone.

Tears were falling down John's cheeks, as well, but Damie was totally devastated. John said to her, "I love you, Damie."

Unless someone has lost an unborn child, the emotions cannot be imagined. They vary from individual to individual, but they cannot be described. This was the biggest crisis moment that John and Damie had ever shared as husband and wife. This was a moment that their decision to depend on God was crucial to their relationship with each other, and to their relationship with Him.

"Honey, look at me," John said. "God promises all of His children that He causes all things to work together for our good. Not for our constant happiness, but for our eternal good. Despite how we feel right now, there is no reason to think God is a liar, because He never has been, and He never will be. Damie, I love you so very much!"

As they embraced each other again, John cried on Damie's shoulder, while Damie cried on John's shoulder.

Chapter 20

*J*ohn and Damie both took some time off in their busy lives to be with each other, and to be alone with the Father. Damie had talked to Elizabeth personally, but other than that, they refused all contact with the rest of the world. And at this point in time in their lives, that included a lot of people. They both realized that they had become very public figures, and their comments and reactions to the situations in their lives were going to come under much scrutiny. Under no circumstances did they want to say or do the wrong things.

The day was gloomy physically, as well as emotionally for John and Damie. It was cold, cloudy, and snow seemed imminent. John and Damie were both sitting on the sofa in their living room.

Damie said to John, knowing that it was not her alone that was feeling the loss she was feeling, "John, I feel like Hannah Rose is the perfect name for our child, for she has indeed risen to be with Jesus forever. And do you know what else I have realized? Our daughter will never have to deal with the horrors of this life, but instead, from this moment on, she will be in the presence of Jesus, forever with Him in Paradise. And, Honey, do you remember praying for God to keep both Hannah and me safe and well cared for? Can you think of a safer, more cared for place for Hannah to be than in our Savior's arms?"

John was amazed. "Damie, I remember all those years ago, when we were just chatting with each other online, your level of faith in God Almighty amazed me then. I had no idea at what a high level it was or would grow to. You are a truly inspiring vessel that God uses!"

"All glory to God, Sweetie, all glory to God. For in my strength alone, I am a mess. All glory to God!" Damie began to cry again, as would often be the case in the coming days.

"Damie, will you kneel here with me?" John asked.

With tears in his eyes, John prayed, "Father, we come before You, again with praise and thanksgiving. Father God, I do thank You for taking Hannah to where she will never have to experiences the tribulations of this life. Abba, I thank you that You are conforming us into the image of Your son, Jesus. We do, God, as You know, feel a tremendous loss, having not gotten to know Hannah yet, but we know, Father, that the day is coming that we will. Father, I ask You again to keep Damie and I both in the center of Your perfect will, and keep our eyes permanently focused on You. God, we don't understand this life all the time, and we don't know what tomorrow holds, but we thank You for holding our tomorrow! Father, it is with broken hearts that we pray these things, in Your Son Jesus' holy, precious, and perfect name. Amen."

John and Damie thought about Hannah often, but as each day passed, it became easier and easier to be so very glad that all of her eternity will be spent in the loving arms of Jesus.

The two of them spent around two weeks alone with each other, and each separate and also together, alone with the Father. They had both grown up very quickly, and God, through this process, had further refined His servants, John and Damie Smith.

Within two months of this point in time in their lives, John's secretary had scheduled for John 643 speaking engagements over the next forty-two months. John preached with such fire, such compassion, and such sincerity, that he was frequently compared to Billy Graham. John was quoted in The Washington Post as saying, "Thank you very much for the comparison with Dr. Graham, but with all due respect to him, my prayer is to be conformed to the image of Jesus Christ."

Damie frequently led worship at John's preaching engagements, and she continued to record CDs under the Grace Given Records label. Damie and Elizabeth's relationship continued to grow, and Elizabeth had moved into John and Damie's house. (Into her own apartment, of course!) Damie continued to let the Light of Jesus Christ shine through her life to everyone within her circle of influence.

Galatians 5:22-23. "But the fruit of the Spirit is love, joy, peace, patience, kindness, goodness, faithfulness, gentleness, self-control; against such things there is no law."

Grace has been given; *Pursue the Fruit!*

Printed in the United States
134922LV00001B/1/P

9 781438 932897